Contents

About the Author

Charles Dickens was born in England, in 1812, the second of eight children of a debtridden government clerk. Because his family had handled their money poorly, young Charles was sent to work in a London factory at the age of ten. This experience upset him so greatly and left such an impression on him that he later created suffering and abandoned children as the heroes of many of his novels.

An unexpected, small legacy permitted him to break free of the slave factory and return to school. He became a newspaper reporter—a job which helped him to observe people and to create scenes that live in his readers' memories.

With the appearance of *The Pickwick Papers* in 1836 and 1837, Charles Dickens, at age 24,

GREAT ILLUSTRATED CLASSICS

GREAT EXPECTATIONS

Charles Dickens

Adapted by
Mitsu Yamamoto

Illustrations by Brendan Lynch

BARONET
BOOKS

BARONET BOOKS, New York, New York

GREAT ILLUSTRATED CLASSICS

edited by
Malvina G. Vogel

became the most popular novelist in England. This popularity increased with the publication of *David Copperfield, Oliver Twist, A Christmas Carol, A Tale of Two Cities,* and *Great Expectations.*

Like so many of his other books, *Great Expectations* deals with the evil influence of money. It first appeared as a serial in a weekly magazine, with its main character, Pip, telling the story of his life, from the time he is seven until he is an adult. We see Pip's "great expectations" out of life come to pass, as he undergoes a painful change in his values from selfish vanity to sympathy for others.

Much of Charles Dickens' life was spent writing, editing, touring to read his novels, and promoting many charities to help the poor. He was active in all these until his death in 1870.

Pip Visits His Parents' Graves.

CHAPTER 1

Meeting by a Grave

Though I lived most of my early years here in Kent, its marshes can still frighten me. The mists make figures, and strange sounds carry over the river close by. It was no different that one Christmas Eve, when I was seven years old. I was visiting my parents' graves in the churchyard on the deserted marshes. I never really knew my parents, so I could only read their names on the tombstones—Philip and Georgiana Pirrup. Philip is my name too, but when I was learning to talk, I could not pronounce it, so I made it into "Pip"—the name I came to be called all my life. As I tried desperately to remember my parents, I began to cry.

Suddenly, a terrible voice cried, "Stop your noise or I'll cut your throat!"

A huge man appeared from among the graves and seized my chin in a steely grip. He was dressed in coarse gray clothes, with an iron band clamped around one leg. He was wet and shivering and mud-stained, but his eyes glared brightly at me.

I was terror-stricken. "Please, sir, don't kill me!" I pleaded. "Please don't!"

"What's your name? Quick!" he demanded. "And where do you live, you and your folks?"

"Pip is my name, sir," I managed to say. "My parents are there in those graves, and I live with my only sister, Mrs. Joe Gargery, and her husband, the blacksmith, in the village."

"Blacksmith, eh?" he said, looking down at his leg.

Suddenly, in one motion, he turned me upside down and emptied my pockets. A few nails and a piece of bread were all I had in them. Putting me right-side up, on top of a high tombstone, he

"Please, Sir, Don't Kill Me!"

crammed the bread in his mouth and ate it ravenously.

"Now, young villain, I'm deciding if I'll let you live," he said, tilting me backwards. "Do you know what a file is?"

I nodded, too frightened to speak as I clung to the tombstone.

"Well, you get me one—a file and also some food. You bring them here tomorrow morning. You understand me?"

Swallowing hard and clinging to him as he tilted me even more, I gasped, "Yes, sir."

"But you tell anyone and you're a dead boy. I got a friend here who loves cutting the heart out of a boy. That boy may think he's safe in bed, but my friend knows how to sneak into a warm bedroom and find that boy. Remember what I say. Now go!"

I nodded eagerly, then jumped down and ran as fast as I could back home, my heart beating so loudly that I could hear it.

Pip Gets Orders.

But at home there was more trouble. As I tiptoed into the kitchen, my brother-in-law Joe, the blacksmith, shook his big blond head at me. "Pip, where you been?" he asked. "She's been out looking for you."

At that moment, the door burst open and my sister stormed in. Mrs. Joe is twenty years older than me and has a hot temper. Without a word, she banged me in the head and threw me at Joe. But Joe stepped in front of me and turned to face my sister as she rushed at me again. She tried to dodge behind Joe, but he's a giant man—gentle, but a giant, and Joe and I turned like the front and back ends of a horse until my sister got tired of chasing me.

Joe smiled at me as soon as the danger was past and drew me to the warm fireplace. Above the sound of my sister slamming pots and dishes, I heard a gun in the distance.

"What's that, Joe?" I whispered.

"That's a warning gun from the prison-ships down on the river. A convict's escaped. That's the

Joe Protects Pip.

second one. The gun fired last night too, to warn us that a robber or murderer was loose."

A shiver went through me at Joe's words.

My sister banged on the table to indicate her impatience, and we hurried to sit down to dinner. She buttered bread for me and Joe, and handed it out. Though Joe was the provider of the bread and butter, he was too good-natured to object to being treated like a child. While my sister complained of all the house cleaning she had been doing in preparation for a party the next day, Christmas Day, I hid my bread in my pocket. In case I couldn't find anything to take from my sister's pantry, I had to be sure to have something to give my waiting convict.

Since my sister never allowed me a candle to light my way to my attic room, I stumbled in the darkness that night, fearing that I, too, would end up on a prison-ship because of the thieving I was planning from my sister's pantry. Once in bed, I imagined a young convict at the foot of my bed, ready to cut out my heart. So I kept the

Pip Hides Bread for the Convict.

bread clutched in my hand all night, ready to show it to him. He did not come, but I kept expecting him, and so I barely slept.

At the first gray light of dawn, I stole downstairs. The creaking steps seemed to call "Stop, thief!" after me. Because of the holiday season, there was much more food in the pantry than I expected. I took some more bread, a hunk of cheese, a pork-pie, and some brandy. This last I poured into an empty bottle and then refilled the brandy bottle with water to make up for what I had taken. I dared take the pork-pie only because it was on a back shelf, so I guessed my sister did not intend to serve it soon.

A door led from the kitchen to Joe's blacksmith forge. I slipped in and selected a heavy file from among Joe's tools. With all these things clutched under my jacket, I ran for the marshes through the heavy morning mist.

Taking Food from the Pantry

A Second Convict Attacks Pip.

CHAPTER 2

The Second Convict

I was not too far from the ruined walls where I was to meet my man when I suddenly saw him. He was sitting with his back to me, his head nodding forward in sleep. I approached him softly and touched him on the shoulder. He instantly jumped up and whirled around. It was not the same man, but another one!

This one was also dressed in gray and wore a leg iron too, but his face was different. He swore at me and aimed a weak blow at my head. It missed me, but it made him stumble, so he must have been ill and cold. Then he ran off into the mist. I was sure he was the friend who cut out boys' hearts.

At the walls I saw the right man, stamping up and down to warm himself. As I took the food and the file from under my jacket, his eyes widened. With a shivering hand, he began to cram down the food. When I brought out the bottle, he said, "What you got there, boy, in that bottle?"

"Brandy, sir. It helps to ward off the chill of the marshes," I replied.

He snatched the bottle from my hand and drank deeply. Then, wiping his mouth with the back of his hand, he said, "Very thoughtful for a boy. You told no one?"

"No, sir, no one. I stole the food."

Nodding with satisfaction, he took large bites of the pork-pie until it was almost all gone.

"I'm glad you're enjoying it," I said, "but aren't you leaving any for him?"

"You mean my friend that cuts out boys' hearts?" he asked slyly. Then he laughed and added, "He won't want any food."

A Starving Man Eats Greedily.

"He looked like he might," I said.

He immediately stopped eating and cried, *"Looked?* You saw him? Where? When?"

I spoke hurriedly, for he had grabbed me by the collar and was glaring at me. "He was d-down there," I stammered and pointed out the direction. "Dressed like you, and with an iron on his leg. There was a gun fired for him last night. Didn't you hear it?"

"I thought so, and then again I didn't. Being alone in these marshes makes you lightheaded. What kind of face did he have?"

The frightened face that had turned toward me with a gasp reappeared again in my mind. "He had bruises on one cheek," I replied.

The man drew in his breath with a rasp. "So it *is* him! I'll hunt him down like a bloodhound. Where's the file? Give me the file, boy!"

I picked up the file from the ground where he had thrown it when he grabbed the food. Now, pushing aside the rest of the pork-pie, he seized

"He Was D-Down There."

the file from me, knelt on the wet grass, and began to file at his leg iron like a madman.

I said that I had to leave, but he paid no attention to me. I took a few steps backward to see if he would stop me. When he didn't look up, I turned and slipped quietly away. Then I started to run toward home. In the distance I could still hear him filing . . . filing . . . filing . . .

At home, my sister was going around like a whirlwind, putting up clean white curtains and taking the dust covers off the furniture in the parlor. This room was used only on very special occasions, and Christmas was one of them.

Joe and I had to eat breakfast standing up because my sister had no time to set a proper table. Before we were finished eating, she had begun preparing dinner, for guests were expected.

My heart suddenly stopped beating for a moment—could the pork-pie have been meant for today's festivity? This horrible fear stayed with me as my sister washed my face and ears with

Filing at the Leg Iron

her usual rough hand. Soon Joe and I were sitting, stiff and uncomfortable, in our best clothes in the parlor.

At the first knock on the front door, I opened it wide to admit Mr. Wopsle, the clerk of our church. Next came Mr. and Mrs. Hubble, the wheelmaker and his wife. Last, in his own small carriage, came Uncle Pumblechook, who was really Joe's uncle, although my sister had taken him over as a relation because he was a well-to-do seed merchant in town. She welcomed him warmly.

"Mrs. Joe," said Uncle Pumblechook, "I have brought you some wine as a compliment of the season—sherry and port." He said this as if it were a great surprise, but since he brought the same gift every year, it surprised no one.

Dinner was a gay affair for everyone except me. I was not allowed to speak. Much of the conversation centered on me and the burden I was to my poor sister. Joe was not allowed to deny this, but he tried to make it up to me by pouring large

Stiff and Uncomfortable at Christmas

quantities of gravy on my meat. Soon what I had been dreading happened.

My sister said, "Uncle Pumblechook, I have made a special favorite of yours, a pork-pie."

The applause of eager appetites followed her as she left for the pantry. I heard her moving about there, then there was a silence. She returned to us empty-handed, saying, "Goodness gracious! I don't understand it—the pie is gone!"

I could stand it no longer. I had to escape. I jumped up from the table and rushed to the door. As I reached it, it swung open and a party of soldiers entered. I ran blindly into the leader, who called, "Here you are, lad. Come on." And he held a pair of handcuffs out toward me!

"The Pie Is Gone!"

The Soldiers Ask For Help.

CHAPTER 3

Capture and Confession

I stumbled backward from the soldier, thinking, "They know I'm a thief and have come for me."

Joe grabbed my arm and kept me from falling.

The soldier smiled at me, then looked around. "Excuse us, ladies and gentlemen," he said. "I am a sergeant in the service of the king. My men and I are on a hunt for convicts and need the services of the blacksmith."

"That's the blacksmith," said my sister before Joe could speak. "What do you want with him on Christmas Day?"

"We need these handcuffs fixed. The lock is out of line. They will be required soon."

My sister motioned Joe forward, and he examined the cuffs. "I'll have to light my forge," he said. "The repair may take an hour."

"That's all right," said the sergeant. "We have orders to close in around the convicts on the marshes a little before dusk. So forge away!"

The soldiers entered and stacked their arms in a corner. Then all of them except the sergeant followed Joe—now in his leather apron—into the forge to help speed the work.

Uncle Pumblechook invited the sergeant to the table and poured him some of the wine he had brought as a gift. Soon the party became merry again, while in the background we could hear Joe's hammer.

In return for the repair of the cuffs, the sergeant gave permission for our group to follow behind his soldiers and witness the capture. Only Mr. Wopsle and Joe accepted. Mrs. Joe let me go too, warning her husband, "If you bring the boy

Joe Mends the Handcuffs at His Forge.

back with his head blown to bits by a musket, don't look to me to put it together again!"

We went straight to the churchyard where I had first seen my convict. While the soldiers searched, I began to worry that the convict would think I had betrayed him and brought the soldiers to this spot. When they found nothing, we moved on.

By now, a bitter sleet had begun pelting us. Suddenly, a shout sounded in the distance. With a sweep of his hand, the sergeant commanded his men to run toward it. More shouts came from the same direction. Since I could not keep up with the long strides of the men, Joe swept me onto his broad back and hurried after the soldiers. As we got close to a ditch from which water was splashing and mud was flying, we heard the sergeant shouting, "Surrender, you two! Come apart!"

The soldiers stood at the top of the ditch, their muskets leveled at two struggling figures. When the men refused to obey, the soldiers dropped into

Pursuing the Escaped Convicts

the ditch and dragged them out, bloody and panting.

My convict was in a rage as he and the other man were both handcuffed. "Remember," he shouted, "I took him! I gave him to you!"

The other convict, the one with the bruised face, was badly battered and had to be helped to stand. "He tried to murder me!" he gasped.

My convict snorted. "If I *tried,* I would have succeeded. No, I wanted him alive so I could turn him in. I dragged him back here for you." And he pointed to the sergeant. "You don't see any iron on my leg, do you? I could have got clear away, but when I knew *he* was going free as well, I refused to let that happen. I wouldn't let him profit by my means of escape, or be free to get me in trouble again."

"Enough!" ordered the sergeant.

Torches were lit and guns were fired as a signal to the prison-ship to send a boat. In the flickering light of the torches, my convict caught sight of me. I looked at him eagerly and moved my hands

Captured!

slightly and shook my head, trying to assure him that I had not led the soldiers here. His eyes gazed into mine for a moment with a look that I could not understand.

Soon, we began the march to the river, where the convicts were led to the boat.

Just before going aboard, my convict suddenly stopped and turned to the sergeant. "I want to say something," he said clearly so all could hear. "I stole some food and brandy from the blacksmith's house in the village. It was a pork-pie that I took."

Joe said, "Why, my wife just missed that before we came out here. But we don't begrudge a starving man some food, do we, Pip?"

I shook my head, unable to speak.

The convicts stepped into the boat and were rowed to the prison-ship. The rest of us went home.

"I Stole Some Food and Brandy."

Pip Works with Joe in the Forge.

CHAPTER 4

Miss Havisham's Invitation

Joe could not read at all, but then, reading was not required of a blacksmith. I, however, could read a little, and since I was to be apprenticed to Joe when I was old enough, it was plain that I was already educated above my station in life. I wanted nothing more than to be a blacksmith and work with Joe, whom I loved and who loved me and protected me against my sister's temper, as much as he was able. Frequently, his interference in my punishments earned us both a fierce rapping on the head by my sister's hand. And she scolded us equally too.

GREAT EXPECTATIONS

It was shortly after Christmas that a great change came into my life. Uncle Pumblechook arrived one day with an invitation from Miss Havisham—an immensely rich and grim old lady who lived in a big, neglected house. I had never seen the lady, only heard about her. She lived a life of seclusion, and the house was barricaded for fear of robbers. Now this strange woman wanted me to come and play at her house.

Joe was astonished. "How could she have come to know Pip?" he asked Mrs. Joe.

"Noodle!" cried my sister. "Who said she knew him?" She gestured with a smile at Uncle Pumblechook. "Your uncle is her tenant. And one day, when he was paying his rent, he was asked if he knew any boy who could come and play. Out of the goodness of his heart, he mentioned this one here. Now get out of my way so I can clean him up."

With that, she seized me, and soaped and scrubbed and rinsed and toweled me until I shone. Then she brought out fresh underwear

Uncle Pumblechook's Startling News

and my best suit. As I was undergoing this torture, my sister and Uncle Pumblechook dreamed aloud.

She said, "Oh, if only I were a boy and be-friended by a rich woman! It could be the making of him, Uncle, the making of us all!"

Uncle Pumblechook nodded gravely. "No doubt about it. No doubt about it. A fortune may have its eyes on him right now."

In no time at all I was bundled into Uncle's carriage, on my way to play. I dared not ask why or what I should play at, and before I could ask anything at all, we drove up to a locked gate surrounding an old, dismal brick house with many walled-up and barred windows.

Uncle rang the gate bell. A window was raised and a clear voice called out, "What name?"

"Pumblechook delivering a boy, Pip."

The window was closed, and in a few moments a beautiful young girl came across the courtyard

Arriving at Miss Havisham's Gate

to the gate with keys in her hand. She was about my age, but she seemed older because of the proud and haughty way she held her head and shoulders. She scarcely looked at me, but said, "Come in, Pip," and started to close the gate.

When Uncle tried to follow me in, she stopped him with a sharp "Did you wish to see Miss Havisham?"

Uncle Pumblechook looked uncomfortable. "If Miss Havisham wishes to see me," he said.

"Ah," said the girl, "but she doesn't." And she slammed the gate shut.

Leaving Uncle with his dignity severely ruffled, we crossed the courtyard and went into the house through a side door, the front one being chained shut.

It was dark inside, but the girl had left a candle burning on a table by the door. She led me down several passages and up a staircase, saying scornfully several times, "Don't loiter so, boy, or you'll get lost!"

Estella Slams the Gate Shut.

We finally stopped before a closed door and she said, "Go in."

More out of shyness than politeness, I answered, "After you, miss."

"Don't be ridiculous, boy. I'm not going in." And she walked away, taking the candle with her and leaving me alone in the dark hall.

Uncomfortable and half-afraid, I knocked on the door. A cracked voice told me to enter, which I did, and found myself in a large room, lit with candles. It seemed to be a lady's dressing room, for there was a large gilded mirror sitting atop a draped table. Dresses were scattered about on half-packed trunks. In the midst of all this sat the strangest lady I had ever seen. She was dressed all in white—silk, satin, and lace—a bridal gown. A long white bridal veil streamed from her hair, which was white too. Only one of her white shoes was on her feet; the other lay on a table nearby. White gloves, a white lace handkerchief, and a white prayer book sat scattered on her dressing table. Although I say all these things were white,

The Strangest Lady Pip Has Ever Seen

the truth is they had been white once, but were now yellow with age. And age had changed the figure in the wedding dress too, for the dress had obviously been made for a young woman and now hung loose on the woman who had shrunk to skin and bones. This, then, was Miss Havisham.

"Who are you?" she said.

"Pip, ma'am, Mr. Pumblechook's nephew, come to play."

"Come closer," commanded Miss Havisham. "You are not afraid of a woman who has never seen the sun since you were born, are you?"

I shook my head "no," though it was untrue.

She put a hand on her chest on the left side. "Do you know what lies under here?"

"Your heart, ma'am," I managed to say.

"Broken!" She pronounced the word with a weird smile and somewhat boastfully. Then she motioned me to look at her watch on the dressing table and at a clock on the wall. Both said twenty minutes to nine and had stopped. She nodded meaningfully at me. "I am tired and I want to be

Miss Havisham Tells of Her Broken Heart.

amused. I have a sick fancy to see someone play," she said. "Play!"

I could do nothing but stand there, for I didn't know what to do, how to play.

She turned to look at herself in the mirror and, after a while, said impatiently, "Call Estella! You can at least do that, if you can't play, can't you? I say call Estella!"

I went out into the dark corridor and called, and soon Estella's candle came towards me. Miss Havisham beckoned the girl to come to her, then she picked up a jewel from the dressing table and held it against Estella's brown hair.

"It will be yours one day, my dear," she said with a strange laugh. "It will help you to trap the admiration of men and break their hearts. Now play cards with this boy as I watch."

Estella was indignant. "Play with this boy! He's only a common laboring boy!"

I overheard Miss Havisham whisper, "Even so, you can break his heart, can't you?"

A Jewel for Estella's Hair

Estella obeyed, and we sat down to a game of Beggar My Neighbor. But I could not concentrate on the cards. Estella kept up a stream of remarks to Miss Havisham: "What coarse hands he has! And what thick boots!" Soon she laughed with disdain. "See how he calls the knaves by the wrong name. He calls them 'jacks.'"

I was so upset that I misdealt and was called clumsy. Of course, Estella won the game.

Miss Havisham had sat like a corpse as we played, but finally she leaned forward and said to me, "Estella has said many hard things about you, but you say nothing about her. What do you think of her? Tell me."

At her insistence, I whispered in her ear, "Estella is very proud and very pretty . . . and very insulting. Please may I go home now?"

Miss Havisham did not let me leave until the next game was over, but then I was dismissed and told to return in six days' time. Estella was ordered to give me something to eat, which she did—some bread and meat. I felt as if I were a dog

Estella Makes Fun of Pip's Boots.

being fed. All the hurt and humiliations made my tears fall. When Estella saw my reddened eyes, a smile of delight came to her face, and she gave her head a toss of contempt.

My sister was nicer to me that night, for she felt I had come up a little in the world. But I was miserable. I had not known before how common a person I was until Estella had pointed it out. I saw now how thick my boots were. I saw how coarse my hands were. And I saw how ignorant I was, for I had called knaves "jacks." I knew how common I was, and I was ashamed of it because of the beautiful Estella. That day, that meeting with Estella, changed my life completely.

Feeling Like a Dog Being Fed!

Miss Havisham's Dining Room

CHAPTER 5

My First Kiss

Obediently, I returned to Miss Havisham's six days later, and again an arrogant Estella led me along the dark passageway.

Miss Havisham, seated as before at her dressing table, greeted me with, "You do not play very well, boy. Are you willing to work?" At my nod, she directed me to wait for her in the dining room across the hall.

Like her dressing room, this room also had curtains drawn against the daylight and was filled with an oppressive, airless smell. The clocks here, as in the other room, had stopped at twenty minutes to nine. The main piece of furniture was a long table with a dusty, rotting cloth spread on it, as if in preparation for a feast. In the center of the table was a tarnished silver stand that seemed to be the center of activity for speckled-legged spiders. Atop the stand was a yellow mound so heavy with cobwebs that I could not recognize what it was.

I was so fascinated with watching several mice scuttling around the room that I did not hear Miss Havisham hobble in, leaning on a walking stick. She pointed with the stick to the yellow mound under the cobwebs and explained, "That is my bridal cake." Then, putting her twitching hand on my shoulder, she ordered, "Now for your work. You will walk me around."

With her leaning on my shoulder, we walked slowly around and around the room. This, then, was my work, to be followed by a game of cards with Estella under Miss Havisham's eye, and by a dog-like meal.

"That Is My Bridal Cake."

For eight or more months this was the pattern of my visits. In time, I grew less clumsy at play, but Estella was always cruel to me, finding new imperfections in me to laugh at. Only twice was there some difference in the routine.

On one occasion a gentleman was coming down the stairs as Estella was leading me up them. He stopped and looked at me. "Whom have we here?" he asked.

"Just a boy," said Estella carelessly.

He was a large man with a large head. It was hard to feel at ease, for he looked at me with a suspicious gaze under bushy, black eyebrows. "From the neighborhood?"

"Yes, sir," I replied. "I'm Pip, sir."

He thought over my answer, then waved me on. I forgot him, for at that time he was nothing to me.

The other incident that disturbed our routine happened when Miss Havisham had made Estella and me play longer than usual at cards. Usually I was made stupid by nervousness. This

A Man Asks About Pip.

time, having longer to adjust to the card-playing, I did fairly well and Miss Havisham even praised me. This must have made an impression on Estella, for when she saw me to the gate, she turned and said, "Come here! You may kiss me if you like."

I kissed her cheek as she turned it to me. Until that moment, I would have given any thing to kiss Estella, but she had spoken in the same imperious way that Miss Havisham had praised me. She was imitating the old lady, giving a tip to a common boy who had surprisingly done something well. I could not value such a kiss.

One day, Miss Havisham remarked as she placed her arm on my shoulder for her walk, "You are growing tall, Pip." Later she asked if the blacksmith still wanted me as his apprentice. When I told her that it was Joe's dearest wish, she said, "Then it is time for it to become fact. Let me see the papers."

My sister, Joe, and Uncle Pumblechook took me to the Town Hall, and I was registered as Joe's

"You May Kiss Me If You Like."

apprentice. When I brought the papers to Miss Havisham, she nodded in approval and gave me the magnificent sum of twenty-five guineas.

"You have been a good boy," she said. "Here is your reward. Expect no other. You are not to come here again. Joe Gargery is your master now."

When I showed the reward at home, my sister was more convinced than ever that Miss Havisham had plans for me. Uncle Pumblechook agreed and reminded us that it was through him that I had met Miss Havisham.

Joe was in a whirl of delight that I was at last his apprentice. Once it had been my fondest hope too, but now I dreaded facing the forge and life as a blacksmith. Miss Havisham and Estella, their riches and refinement, had changed me permanently!

A Reward from Miss Havisham

Pip is Depressed.

CHAPTER 6

Depressed and Ashamed!

As my apprenticeship with Joe progressed, my depression over it did not stop. My worst fear, unlikely though it was, now became the one of Estella looking in a forge window and seeing me with black face and hands. How she would laugh at me and despise me! I think I would have run away to sea, but I could not hurt Joe by doing such a contemptible thing. Nor could I disillusion his belief that being a blacksmith was a fine thing. Still, I managed not to show any of my unhappiness to Joe, for which I am very glad.

GREAT EXPECTATIONS

When a year had passed, I could no longer fight my desire to see Estella and Miss Havisham once more. Joe was agreeable to my taking a day off, and I soon found myself in front of that familiar gate. It took some time for me to work up the courage to ring, but finally I did so.

A woman answered the bell at the gate and introduced herself as one of Miss Havisham's cousins. I'm certain that the woman would have liked to send me away, but did not dare do so on her own, so she went to ask what to do.

Miss Havisham ordered me in, and I found her and everything else about the rooms unchanged. "Well," she said, "I hope you don't want anything, for you'll get nothing!"

"No, Miss Havisham," I replied. "I only wanted you to know that I am doing well in my apprenticeship, and I am grateful to you for urging it."

"Well, if that is the case, fine!" she said. "You may come to see me now and then. Come on your birthday."

Miss Havisham's Cousin Admits Pip.

When she saw me looking around, she smiled slyly and added, "You're wondering where Estella is, aren't you?"

"Yes, ma'am, I sort of was. I was just hoping she was well."

"She is well and gone abroad. She is being educated as a lady. She is prettier than ever and much admired by all who see her. Do you feel that you have lost her?" She broke into malicious, disagreeable laughter after this question.

I didn't know how to answer, but I didn't have to. She waved me out of the room, and I hurried down the stairs, out of the house, and into the road, her laughter still ringing behind me.

Since I had to walk, it was night by the time I neared home. I could see that the house and the forge were brightly lit, and as I got closer, I saw a crowd of people milling about in the front yard. I started to run, and the crowd parted for me when they saw who I was.

A circle of people stood in the kitchen, Joe and the village doctor among them. As I burst into the

Pip Hopes For News About Estella.

room, they looked up and moved aside so I could see what it was they stood around.

My sister lay on the kitchen floor, not moving, unconscious, and bleeding heavily from her head.

Joe put his arm around me and explained, "Now, old chap, we must be brave. Some villain has crept into this very kitchen and laid out Mrs. Joe with a wicked blow."

"Is she alive, Joe?" I gasped.

The doctor spoke up. "Alive, yes. In her right senses, probably not."

By now, the police were questioning everybody, but no one had seen the attack. Someone had come up behind her as she stood at the stove and dealt her a heavy blow on the back of her head. Though the investigation continued for weeks, the attacker was not found.

Joe and I said nothing to one another, but each of us knew that my sister had made many enemies with her sharp tongue and quick temper. I was not the only person in the village who had received a battering from her strong fists. We

Pip's Sister Has Been Attacked.

knew, but never said, that many people hated her and that any one of them could have dealt her the blow.

She was alive, but her recovery was slow. She never did recover her power of speech or her memory. And her personality was much changed. She was patient and quiet, asking with her hands only to be made warm and comfortable by the fire, like an aged cat.

Joe was much upset by this change in Mrs. Joe, but gradually he became conscious of a quiet and pleasantness in his life that he had never experienced before. This was enhanced because Biddy came to live with us and take care of us.

Biddy was an orphan girl in the village and was distantly related to Mr. Wopsle. She was wonderfully clever, and my reading and writing improved very fast under her guidance. As for her cooking, Joe and I had never tasted such delicious meals. She was gentle and kind with my sister, and kept us all clean and comfortable. For the first time in his life, Joe was able to go freely to

Life Becomes Quiet and Pleasant.

the village pub for a glass of beer and a good talk with the other men.

I found myself confiding in Biddy, for she was sympathetic. But she also had sensible comments to make. So it was to her, not to Joe, that I confided my dream one day. "I want to be a gentleman, Biddy," I said.

She looked up from her sewing. "Because of Estella, is that it? Because she wouldn't want you as you are?"

Miserably, I nodded "yes," ashamed for myself and Estella too.

Pip Confides His Dream to Biddy.

Mr. Jaggers Appears at the Forge.

CHAPTER 7

Great Expectations

I had been an apprentice to Joe for almost four years when Mr. Jaggers appeared at our door. I recognized him immediately as the man Estella and I had met on the stairs at Miss Havisham's years before. There was no mistaking those sharp, suspicious eyes and bushy, black eyebrows.

He spoke with great authority. "I have reason to believe I am facing the blacksmith, Joseph Gargery, and his apprentice, Pip."

"Quite right, sir," answered Joe.

"My name is Jaggers, and I am a lawyer in London, sent to you by one of my clients."

Joe was impressed by the grandeur of this speech, and he led the way into the parlor. I followed, snatching off the dust covers from a table, a chair, and the sofa.

Mr. Jaggers took the chair by the table and, looking sternly at Joe, began to speak. "I am here with an offer to relieve you of your apprentice, Pip. It is to his good. Would you demand to be paid to let him go?"

"No, I want nothing, and I would not stand in Pip's way," Joe quickly replied.

Jaggers turned to me. "My instructions are to inform you that eventually you will come into property and money. The person from whom these riches will come wants you to be ready and able to use them. Therefore, this person wishes you to be educated and brought up as a gentleman, with great expectations of wealth."

An Offer of Great Expectations.

I caught my breath. Here was my dream come true! Miss Havisham was going to make my wild fancy a reality.

"Now, Mr. Pip," continued Jaggers, "there are conditions. First, this person wishes you to always bear the name of Pip. Second, the name of your benefactor will remain a secret until that person chooses to reveal it. If you have a suspicion who this person may be, you are not to hint at it, but keep silent. Is that clear?"

I nodded.

"Do you accept?"

I nodded again and assured Mr. Jagger that the conditions were clear and that I would abide by them.

Mr. Jaggers let a few minutes pass to signify how important his last words had been. Then he roused himself. "Now, as to the arrangements. I have said that you have great expetations for your future, but for the present, a very handsome sum of money has already been provided for you. It will be more than enough for your education

Jaggers Sets Down the Conditions.

and living expenses. This money will be handled by me on your behalf. So consider me your guardian."

When I tried to thank him, he held up his hand. "No, no thanks. I am being very well paid for my services. Now, listen closely to my suggestions: You are to come to London immediately after purchasing some suitable clothes. There, you will lodge with one Herbert Pocket, a young gentleman of your own age. Perhaps you will be able to pick up some of the habits and manners of a gentleman from him. And I suggest employing his father as your tutor. What do you say to all this?"

"Yes, of course, Mr. Jaggers, whatever you think best," I said in a rush. "I've heard of the Pockets, for they are related to Miss Havisham."

Mr. Jaggers's face became stonelike. "Yes, I believe that is so. Now, here is some money for the clothes and the journey."

He counted out twenty guineas on the table and added his business card to the money. Then he said good-bye and was gone.

Jaggers Leaves Money and a Business Card.

Joe and I continued to sit on the sofa, stunned. Biddy found us there, as still as two statues. But Joe came to his senses and poured out the story of my good fortune to her, then ran into the kitchen to try to make my sister understand what had happened.

Left alone, Biddy shook my hand heartily, then said quietly, "So one dream is coming true, Pip. I wonder if your others will too."

I knew that she referred to my love for Estella, but I also knew that she thought Estella proud and unworthy. So I only said, "Who knows?"

My sister's mind was now so weak that we were never able to make her understand what had happened. She smiled and nodded, pleased at the extra attention she was getting.

Early the next morning, I went to the shop of Mr. Trabb, the tailor in our village. When his boy told me the tailor was still at breakfast in his apartment behind the shop, I waited impatiently until he called me to his table. He did not think it worth his while to interrupt his meal and come

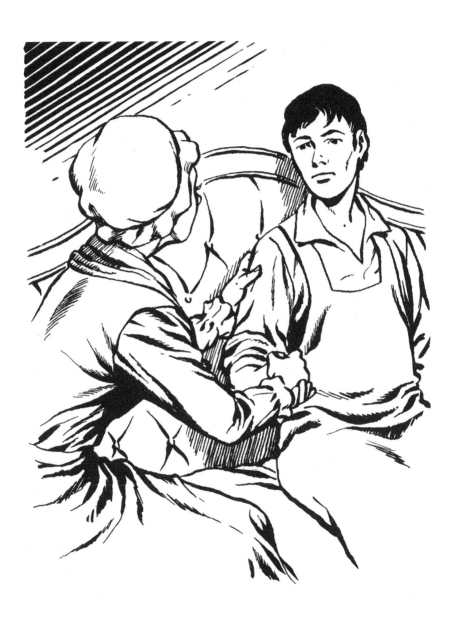

"One Dream Is Coming True, Pip."

out to me, nor did he offer me anything to eat as I stood before him.

"Mr. Trabb," I began, as he went on eating, "I have come into some money."

The tailor stiffened. He put down his buttered roll, wiped his fingers, and got up from his chair. His eyes widened as I took some guineas from my pocket and explained, "I am leaving soon for London, and I want a fashionable suit to wear on the journey."

Mr. Trabb swept me into his shop and started a flurry of activity. His boy was ordered to lift various bolts of cloth from the shelves. Mr. Trabb then unfurled each one, praising them all to me. With his assistance, I selected a cloth fit for a young gentleman. I stood still as he measured me, all the while assuring me that my proportions would make any suit look distinguished. He even opened the door for me himself when I left. This, then, was my first experience with the enormous power of money!

Choosing Cloth for a Fine New Suit

GREAT EXPECTATIONS

When the suit was ready, I wore it to Miss Havisham's to say good-bye. She told me she knew of my good fortune from Mr. Jaggers, and she wished me well. Then she waved me out with her cane. I wanted to thank her, but I remembered Mr. Jaggers's conditions and did not reveal that I believed her to be my benefactor.

Her final words to me were: "Good-bye, Pip! You will always keep the name of Pip, you know."

I nodded, waved, and left.

As the day neared for my departure, Joe grew more and more solemn. Finally he said, "It's not my apprentice that's being took from me, but a little child that's sat with me many a night by the fire and that's watched me many a day at the forge."

I turned away in tears, for I was so eager to leave, so eager for my great expectations to become a reality, that I had forgotten my dearest friend Joe.

Saying Good-Bye to Miss Havisham

Pip Arrives in London.

Chapter 8

My New Life

I made the journey to London in a four-horse stagecoach in about five hours. I would have been frightened at being in such a big city except that I found it dirty and full of ugly, narrow, crooked streets.

I went at once to Mr. Jaggers's office. He told me what my allowance was to be, a sum that seemed enormous to me. He also gave me business cards of tailors and various other tradesmen from whom I could buy on credit, with the bills being sent to Mr. Jaggers. This would be a convenience to me, but also it would allow Mr. Jaggers to keep track of my spending. He then ordered his clerk, Mr. Wemmick, to guide me to the rooms I was to share with young Herbert Pocket.

Mr. Wemmick was a short, dry man, but his eyes were keen and glittering. He led me to Barnard's Inn, a collection of buildings around a courtyard. We passed through a gate, entered one of the buildings, and walked upstairs to rooms on the tip floor. A note was stuck over the mailbox: "Back soon." Since the door was unlocked we went in.

"Well, you won't need me anymore," said Mr. Wemmick. "But since I am in charge of the cashbox for Mr. Jaggers, no doubt we will meet pretty often."

I thanked him and he left. I looked around the rooms that were to be my new home. They were large enough and seemed even larger, for they had little furniture in them. Also, they were not very clean, but then they belonged to a bachelor.

Wemmick Leads Pip to Barnard's Inn.

GREAT EXPECTATIONS

In about twenty minutes I heard footsteps in the hall, and a pale young man entered, carrying a container of strawberries. Half out of breath, he smiled widely and said, "Mr. Pip?"

I smiled back. "Yes, Mr. Pocket."

"I am so sorry I was out, but I wasn't sure what time the stage got in, and it occurred to me that you might like some fresh fruit with your dinner, so I dashed out."

This was the first indication I had of Herbert's kindness. He scarcely heard my thanks for he was rattling on about our living arrangements. The coffee-house in the next building supplied our meals, and I paid for both of us, by Mr. Jaggers's arrangement, because Herbert was poor though he was a gentleman. He confessed this in so cheerful and frank a manner that I liked him more every minute. He was poorly paid in his banking job, and this accounted for the sparse furnishings.

By the time I unpacked, a waiter had brought up a delicious dinner of chicken, melted butter,

Herbert Pocket Welcomes Pip.

cheese, and crusty bread. Perhaps it seemed to me better than it was because I was independent, with no older people around, and I was in London.

I did not know if Herbert knew my story from Jaggers or from Miss Havisham, since he was related to her, but I wanted him to hear it all, and I spent the next hour giving him all the details. I finished by asking him to correct my manners and to show me proper London ways.

In exchange, Herbert told me Miss Havisham's story as we ate. "Her mother died when she was small," he began, "and her father spoiled her. He left her a fortune. By the way, Pip, in London it is not customary to put the knife in the mouth. The fork is used for that purpose. It's a minor suggestion."

He said this last in such a lively manner that I hardly blushed, but rather thanked him.

Herbert continued with his story. "Miss Havisham fell in love with a handsome man, whom my father distrusted. She gave him enormous

Correcting Pip's Manners During Dinner

sums of money during their engagement. But on their wedding day, he sent a letter breaking off the marriage. She received it at—"

I interrupted. "At twenty minutes to nine when she was dressing."

"Exactly," said Herbert. "She stopped all the clocks and everything was kept untouched to this day. A small matter, dear Pip, but it is not necessary to empty your wine glass so deeply that it rests on your nose."

I quickly put my glass down and thanked him again for his correction. Then I asked, "Why didn't he marry Miss Havisham and in that way control all her money?"

"No one knows, but we think he was already married. This showed he had been false the whole time and had never really loved her."

I shook my head. "Poor Miss Havisham!" I said. "My poor benefactor!"

Herbert Tells Miss Havisham's Story.

Meeting Mr. Pocket and Two Students

CHAPTER 9

A Visitor from Home

The next day, Herbert took time off from his job to take me to his father's house and introduce me. My tutor's hair was gray, but his face was youthful. His smile and natural manner were very like Herbert's. I liked him at once. I was to receive my lessons with two other students, whom I then met. Startop was friendly and good-natured, but Bentley Drummle and I disliked one another on sight. I later found that Drummle disliked most everyone because he considered himself too good for ordinary company. He was related to the aristocracy, but his manner was sulky and rude. As I reported to Herbert, Drummle reminded me of a large spider and was just about as pleasant.

Mr. Pocket began at once on my education, which extended to famous sights and places I must visit in London.

One day as I sat looking around my rather depressing rooms at Barnard's Inn, I realized that they didn't have to look as they did. I resolved to surprise Herbert by buying new furniture, rugs, and curtains. When I told Mr. Jaggers of my plan, he laughed.

"I knew it would take no time at all before you'd catch on to city life. How much?"

As I was considering the sum, Mr. Jaggers's housekeeper arrived with a hot lunch for him. She was a tall woman, about forty years old, with large, faded eyes. She did not seem entirely normal, for she kept her eyes on Mr. Jaggers in a pleading way. Yet I could see the lunch was a fine one. I finally named a sum, and Mr. Jaggers called Mr. Wemmick in and instructed him to count it out for me.

Jaggers' Housekeeper Serves Lunch.

Herbert was delighted with the splendid appearance of our rooms and shook my hand several times a day for the next week to express the pleasure he took in them. The redecoration was no sooner finished than I learned I was to have a visitor, one who would be unable to distinguish between my Oriental rug and the ugly carpet in my sister's parlor.

Biddy had written that Joe was set on visiting me, and my return letter confirmed the day. In truth, I didn't want to see him. If I could have paid the dear man to stay away, I would have done so. But how could I tell him that I was no longer the Pip he had once known?

On the appointed day, I heard him clumping up the stairs. When he reached my door, I thought he would never finish wiping his feet. I was about to lift him bodily off the mat, but at last he came in. With his face all aglow, he seized both my hands and worked them straight up and down as if I were some new kind of pump.

Pip Buys Elegant New Furniture.

I offered to take his hat, which I saw was new, but Joe kept hold of it as if it were precious. His eyes rolled around and around the room and around and around the flowered pattern of my dressing gown. Joe was almost tonguetied, and I was glad when Herbert came in, followed by a waiter, who set out a meal.

Before we sat down at the table, Joe was forced to give up his hat. He placed it on the corner of the mantel above the fireplace, from which it fell at intervals.

"Will you have coffee or tea, Mr. Gargery?" asked Herbert, ready to pour out either.

"Thank you, sir," replied Joe, stiff from head to foot, "I'll take whichever is most agreeable to yourself."

"What do you say to coffee, then?"

"Thank you, sir," said Joe, looking a little unhappy. "Since you are so kind as to make a choice of coffee, I will not go contrary to your opinion. But don't you ever find it heats one up a bit?"

Joe Comes for a Visit.

"It shall be tea, then," said Herbert, and he poured it out.

Here, Joe's hat tumbled off the mantel. He leaped to pick it up and return it to the exact same spot.

As he ate, Joe fell into unaccountable fits of meditation with his fork midway between his plate and his mouth. He coughed strangely, and he sat so far from the table that he dropped more food than he ate.

I was very glad when Herbert left us. Of course, it was all my fault. If I had been more relaxed with Joe, he would have been more relaxed with me.

"Us two being now alone, sir—" he began. "Please, Joe," I interrupted almost angrily, "how can you call me sir!"

He looked down and began again. "I was wrong to come here, Pip. I'm wrong in these clothes. I belong in the forge and on the marshes. I know I'm awful dull, but if you should ever want to see old Joe, you come and put your head in the old forge

Joe's Manners Embarrass Pip.

window like you used to do. Now, good-bye, dear old Pip. God bless you, God bless you!"

For several weeks afterward, I was full of shame at myself over dear Joe's visit. This was intensified still further when I received the news that my sister had died. At this, I felt only a kind of relief.

It wasn't until years later, when I was twenty, that I received good news from my past. This came through Mr. Jaggers—and it was glorious! It was from Estella, who had just returned from France. She was coming to live in London, and she invited me to call upon her!

Good News from Estella

Pip's High Spirits Overflow.

CHAPTER 10

Estella

I was so happy that I was to see Estella soon that my high spirits overflowed. I went around singing and laughing and being pleased with everything in life. While this was pleasant for me, I realized that Herbert might find this continual cheerfulness rather tiresome. I apologized to him and shyly confessed that I was in love with Estella.

Instead of being amazed, Herbert replied in a matter-of-fact way, "Yes, I know."

"How . . . how do you know?" I stammered.

"It has been written all over you since you first

told me about your boyhood visits to Miss Havisham's house," replied Herbert.

It was a relief and a pleasure to pour out my admiration of Estella's beauty, my own unworthiness of her love, and my hope to marry her. I confided that Miss Havisham undoubtedly intended that I should marry Estella, or why else would she make a gentleman of me and settle a fortune on me?

Herbert agreed that he, like all Miss Havisham's relatives, assumed that this must be the case. But then a rather somber look came over his face, and he said, "Now, Pip, I am going to say something disagreeable. But first I want you to know that I, too, am in love. Her name is Clara Barley. I want you two to meet, but I mention her now so you will not think that I had any hopes of marrying Estella myself."

No such thought had ever crossed my mind, but I let Herbert continue.

"When Mr. Jaggers laid down the conditions of your great expectations, he did not mention that

Herbert Confesses His Love for Clara.

you were required to marry Estella as one of them, did he?"

I shook my head "no."

"Then you are not bound to her, and I urge you most strongly to detach yourself from loving her."

"But why, Herbert?" I asked, confused.

"Think of her upbringing and how Miss Havisham has managed her thoughts and feelings. Think how proud and cold Estella is—how much like Miss Havisham she is."

I turned away. "I can never detach myself from her!" I cried. "I adore her completely."

This concern for my welfare touched me deeply, though his words about Estella's character upset me and stayed with me for a long while.

It was about this time that I turned twenty-one, and Mr. Jaggers gave the handling of my money into my own hands. He had allowed me to go into debt to a certain extent, but now I was resolved to live on my splendid income of

Herbert Warns Pip Against Estella.

five hundred pounds a year. I also received a birthday gift of five hundred pounds from my benefactor.

Secretly, with Mr. Wemmick's help, I used half that sum to buy a position for Herbert in a newly established shipping business. An honest and clever young man named Clarriker owned the firm, and he needed additional money and intelligent help. I contracted to make further payments in time, so that Herbert would one day become a full partner.

When Herbert told me of a "chance" meeting with Clarriker and the offer of a position, his ecstatic face was reward enough for me. Herbert need never know who *his* benefactor was, and he grew happier day by day in his new career.

Estella, meanwhile, had become an instant success in London and was enjoying every minute of it. Miss Havisham had arranged for her to live with a widow, who had a daughter about Estella's age. This family was well-bred and had many

Herbert Gets a Position with Clarriker.

society connections. Because of this, Estella began to call on me constantly to escort her to balls and parties and shopping.

I should have been happy, but I wasn't. She treated me like a half-brother or like her secretary. Even though her many admirers were jealous of my position at her side, she showed me no favors. Instead, she said to me one evening, "Pip, oh, Pip, will you never listen to any warnings about me?"

"Do you mean warnings against being attracted to you, Estella?" I asked.

"If you don't know what I mean, you are blind," she replied.

I would have said that love *is* blind, but I always hesitated to press my love on her since I knew she would obey Miss Havisham, and I hated to act like a burden on her. So I was not happy.

But in the next breath, she ordered me to escort her to see Miss Havisham, who wanted her to visit, but disliked her traveling alone.

Pip Escorts Estella to a Ball.

GREAT EXPECTATIONS

As we sat by the fire after dinner, Miss Havisham could not take her eyes off Estella. She had a witch-like eagerness to hear about Estella's conquests from her own lips, for Estella wrote her regularly, and Miss Havisham already knew the names of discarded suitors.

When I saw Miss Havisham's eyes glitter with evil delight over this, I realized that this was her revenge on men, revenge on the man who had left her on their wedding day.

Miss Havisham grasped Estella's hand, eager to hear more, but when Estella pulled her hand away, the old lady had a taste of her own medicine. Terribly hurt, she cried out, "Estella, you are tired of me!"

Estella, with a composed face and calm tone, answered, "I am only tired of myself."

"You stone! You cold heart!" screamed Miss Havisham, waving her stick about.

"You have trained me to be that way," stated Estella.

"You Cold Heart!"

"But not to me," cried Miss Havisham. "Only to them! You must love me, as I love you."

Estella shook her head. "Mother by adoption, I owe everything to you. I will do anything you ask, but I cannot do the impossible. You taught me to be cold and hard. You taught me not to love. I have learned your lessons well."

I could not watch the scene any longer, and I left the two women and went into the garden. But even there, Miss Havisham's moans and pleadings reached my ears.

"You Taught Me Not To Love."

Bills, Bills, and More Bills!

CHAPTER 11

My Benefactor Is Revealed

As the time passed after my twenty-first birthday, I was unable to keep the resolve that I had made then: to stay out of debt and live on the five hundred pounds a year from my benefactor. In addition to the money I owed to Clarriker to complete the contract I had made on Herbert's behalf, I owed my tailor, wine merchant, jeweler, and many others. But I hoped that with every birthday, larger properties would be transferred to me from my benefactor, whereby I would be able to pay all my debts at once. Then I would live in a really grand and expensive manner.

GREAT EXPECTATIONS

I was twenty-three now and laughed at the Pip of twenty-one who had thought five hundred pounds a year a great fortune. I never thought of the Pip who was once convinced that being a blacksmith in Kent was the most desirable position in the world.

I was no longer tutored, but instead read regularly many hours a day. On one particular night, I was at home reading because Herbert was away on a business trip and the weather was too stormy for me to go out. The clock at St. Paul's Cathedral struck eleven, disturbing my concentration. Then footsteps on the stairs disturbed it even more.

Because the wind had blown out the lamps on the staircase, I took my reading lamp to the door. As my light flashed into the entryway, the footsteps stopped.

I looked down the staircase, calling out, "Who's there? What do you want?"

"I'm a-looking for Mr. Pip," answered a man, coming up into the light. When he saw me, this

Pip Hears Footsteps on the Stairs.

stranger's face lit up. His clothes were rough, but good enough, and he had long, iron-gray hair. I guessed he was about sixty, though he had a large, muscular body. As he came level with me, he held out his sunburned hands.

I didn't know what to make of this and said, "Yes, I'm Pip. What is it? What business do you have with me?"

"Ah, yes, my business. I'll explain."

He paused, and I understood that he expected to be invited in. I did so in an abrupt manner, for I didn't understand the happiness that shone from his face and that seemed to demand the same response from mine. He looked about the parlor with a gratified smile, then held out his hands to me again. I began to suspect he might be mad, so I backed away.

"Ah, I understand," he said. "It's not your fault. But it's a disappointing reception after I've come so far and looked forward so much to this meeting with you."

A Stranger Arrives.

GREAT EXPECTATIONS

The man threw off his coat and hat and sat in a chair by the fire. Stretching out his hands to the flames and looking over his shoulder at me, he asked, "Anyone around?"

"What right do you have to ask me that!" I returned heatedly. "You, a stranger coming into my rooms at this time of night?"

He shook his head and grinned with affection. "You're a brave one!" he cried. "I'm glad you growed up to be a brave one."

And then, like a bolt of lightning, it came to me who he was—my convict from the churchyard in the marshes of Kent!

He saw the recognition in my face and came to me, again with his hands outstretched. Hardly realizing that I was doing it, I put out my hands. He grasped them heartily, then kissed them.

"You acted nobly, my boy," he said. "And I have never forgot that noble Pip."

As he was about to embrace me, I held a hand against his chest and pushed him away.

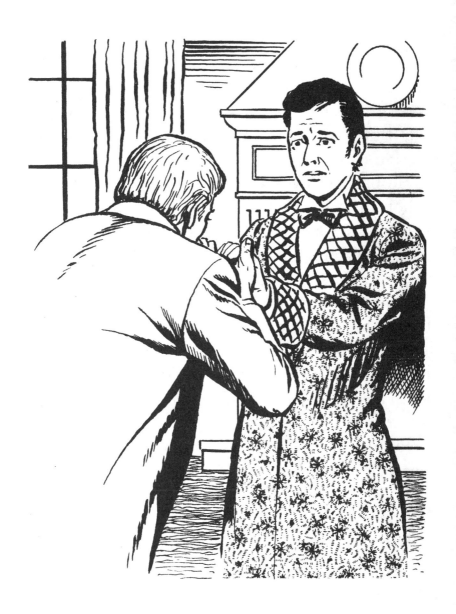

"I Have Never Forgot That Noble Pip."

"If you have come to thank me, it was not necessary," I said. "If I helped you as a child, I hope your gratitude has led you to a reformed way of life. But in any case, I cannot offer you any protection now."

He backed away from me and looked around. When his eyes rested on the row of bottles on a sideboard, I said at once, "But perhaps you will have a warming drink before you leave?"

"Aye, whisky," he said, sitting down.

I served both of us, then said, "How have you been living these past years?"

"I've done wonderful well in New South Wales," he said. "I'm a sheep farmer. And can I be so bold as to ask how you have done since we were shivering on them marshes?"

Reluctantly, I told him my story. When I finished, he said quietly, "May I guess at your income since you came of age? I would say five hundred pounds a year."

He was looking at me steadily. Though he spoke softly, his words entered my being like a

"I've Done Wonderful Well."

scream and I trembled.

"I suppose someone has been taking care of all this, a go-between?" he asked. "And would the first initial of that person's name be 'J'?"

I could not speak. I felt as if I were suffocating, and gripped a table for support. And still he went on.

"In fact, isn't that person's name Jaggers? And his clerk's name Wemmick?"

My head was now reeling so, that I had to feel my way to the sofa, where I fell back into the cushions. He helped me sit up, then dropped on one knee before me.

"Yes, Pip, dear boy, I've made a gentleman of you!" he exclaimed. "It's me what has done it! I swore that every cent I earned should go to you. And then when I began to earn pounds, I lived rough so you should live smooth."

I shrank away from him as if he were some terrible beast. I dreaded him.

He went on. "You're more to me than a real son could be, Pip. Many a lonely night, after herding

"I've Made a Gentleman of You!"

the sheep, I'd be eating my solitary meal and your face would come to me. And I'd say to myself, 'Here's the boy again, a-looking at me while I eats and drinks like he done on the marshes.' And then I'd swear again I'd make a gentleman of you that put life back in me once. And I done it!" He looked around with pleasure at the Oriental rug, the paintings, my elegant clothes, the ruby ring I wore, and the books.

I sat speechless as he went on. "I'm famous for having pulled myself up in New South Wales. They point me out behind my back for the convict I been. But only I knew that I owned a gentleman, which is more than any of them did. What kept me going was I knew someday I'd come back to see my boy and make myself known to him."

In his triumph and excitement, he did not notice how I dreaded his touch and with what misery I received his revelations. Finally he said, "Where will I sleep, dear boy? I've had a long, dangerous journey."

"I Pulled Myself Up in New South Wales."

"My roommate is away. You can have his bed," I said when my voice returned. "But how do you mean 'dangerous'?"

"The authorities will hang me if they find me back in London," he said simply.

I immediately closed all the curtains and led him to Herbert's room, sick at heart that he had risked his life to see me. And also sick at heart because I could not feel any tenderness for him.

Before I left him for the night, I asked, "Then there was no other but you?"

He looked at me in surprise. "No, dear boy, only me."

There went my dream of Estella. So Miss Havisham had *not* singled me out to be Estella's husband. I was just her useful escort, someone to play with cruelly as the old woman had trained her to do. I sat looking into the dying fire until far into the morning, more wretched than I had ever been.

Dreams Go Up in Smoke.

Pip Pretends an Uncle is Visiting.

CHAPTER 12

Helping Abel Magwitch

My convict's name was Abel Magwitch. He had met Mr. Jaggers when that lawyer defended him. Jaggers had kept him from being hanged, but only on the condition that he leave England and go to New South Wales in Australia and settle there.

Magwitch's arrival brought new problems. I decided to face one problem at a time. I told my snooping landlady that my uncle had arrived. But with Herbert soon to return from his business trip, I would have to find other rooms for Magwitch.

The next morning, he ate a huge breakfast with enjoyment and afterwards lit up his pipe with a black, evil-smelling tobacco. "Pip," he said, "you must have horses of your own, and a carriage, and a servant to drive you."

He tossed a purse overflowing with money on the table and said, "Now here's something worth spending, dear boy. And there's more where that come from. I've come to see my gentleman spend his money *like* a gentleman. That will be *my* pleasure."

I stopped him with a raised hand. "This is not what we should be talking about. We must discuss how to keep you safe while you are here. How long will you be staying?"

He looked at me with surprise. "Why, dear boy, I've come for good!" he exclaimed. "Dyed hair and spectacles and elegant clothes will disguise me and keep me safe."

I persuaded him that a prosperous farmer's outfit would suit his sunburned face and work-worn hands much better.

Magwitch Insists That Pip Spend Money.

Before buying the clothes, I went to Mr. Jaggers's office. He and Mr. Wemmick exchanged a look as I entered, and before I could utter a word, Jaggers warned, "No names!"

"Yes, Mr. Jaggers. I have a visitor from New South Wales. He says he is my benefactor. Is that the truth?" I asked.

"It is the truth," said Jaggers.

Desperately I said, "I always supposed it was Miss Havisham. You let me think so."

"No," objected Jaggers. "I did not. Miss Havisham may have encouraged this fanciful idea of yours, but it was just an amusement in her sick mind."

I was now completely convinced that Magwitch was my benefactor, and I hurried home to rent rooms for him near my own. I brought back the farmer's clothes, but they did little to make him look like an ordinary citizen.

That night, he fell asleep in an armchair in his new outfit. I watched him and wanted more than anything in the world to run away, out of the

Jaggers Confirms Magwitch's Story.

room, out of London, out of the country. But I stayed, longing for the moment when Herbert would return and advise me.

Magwitch would not permit me to tell Herbert about him until he had seen him and made a judgment about his trustworthiness. But Herbert had not been home more than five minutes before Magwitch nodded to me and took out a worn Bible on which to swear Herbert to secrecy.

After I had taken Magwitch to his new rooms, Herbert and I talked late into the night. I poured out all I had been thinking, then made a decision. "I will not take another cent from Magwitch, even though I am deeply in debt and not trained for any profession. The money belongs to a criminal!"

Herbert shook his head. "I understand how you feel, Pip, but you will destroy him if you refuse his money. That is what he has lived for. I believe he would give himself up if you do not buy a carriage and horses."

"I will not get in deeper with him!" I cried

Herbert is Sworn to Secrecy.

passionately. "I will not spend his money. I just want him to leave."

"Then if you do not want to be responsible for his capture and his hanging," said Herbert, "you must persuade him to leave England.'

"But he won't!" I cried.

"Then you must go with him."

I looked at Herbert, shocked.

He continued, "When you have gotten him safely away, then break with him, and come back and work with me at Clarriker's."

I decided that this was the only answer.

While I was in the midst of making all these arrangements, Estella summoned me to her home. "I am going to be married soon," she said coolly. "I warned you, you know."

When she told me the groom was to be Bentley Drummle, whom I thought of as a repulsive spider, I protested vigorously.

Estella, however, shrugged her shoulders and said, "It is a suitable match. He is wealthy, and I have decided on it."

Estella Announces Her Marriage Plans.

In a State of Despair!

CHAPTER 13

A Murderess!

After leaving Estella, I walked around London in a state of despair. Though I was no longer in a financial position to ask her to be my wife, it was especially bitter that her choice had fallen on the sulky Drummle. Even though she had said, with a cynical smile, "Don't imagine that I shall make him happy," this was no comfort to me.

Returning very late to my rooms, I opened the door, only to see a figure jerk out of sleep in a chair by the fire. We were both startled, but in a moment I saw it was Mr. Wemmick. He put his finger to his lips in an indication of silence and motioned me closer.

"Forgive me for startling you, Mr. Pip," he said in a low voice. "Mr. Herbert gave me the key. Now beyond that, we will not use any names. You understand?"

I nodded, my heart beginning to beat very fast. "Is something wrong?" I whispered.

"Yes and no," replied Wemmick.

I threw down my coat and hat and sat down close to Wemmick.

He explained, "You may have noticed that Mr. Jaggers has clients of many kinds—not all of them the best class of people. Far from it. But that kind of person often hears things that you or I would not, since we don't drink in certain low saloons or have friends among the criminal class."

I was about to protest this last comment but thought better of it and kept still.

"One such low person passes on all the gossip he hears to us because he wishes to keep on the good side of Mr. Jaggers in case he must ask for

Wemmick Has News for Pip.

his professional services," continued Wemmick. "Today, we heard that a man named Compeyson is spreading the rumor that a visitor from New South Wales is in London. That rumor is bound to reach the authorities soon."

I paled and felt cold in spite of the heat from the fire. "He must not be captured!" I cried.

"Mr. Jaggers and I agree most heartily," said Wemmick. "Thus, tonight while you were out, Mr. Herbert and I arranged to shift that visitor from his rooms near here to a house by the river. Mr. Jaggers imagined someone might follow you in the hopes of being led to that visitor, so the move was made without you being near." Mr. Wemmick smiled in a satisfied way, then became serious again. "But more remains to be done."

"I know," I said rather wildly. "He must be taken out of London. I have made up my mind to that, and I shall go with him since he will not leave otherwise."

"Good!" pronounced Wemmick. "But these things must not be done hastily. Plans must be

Pip Fears for Magwitch's Safety.

made carefully. Mr. Jaggers is most insistent on that. He will be in touch with you as to when it would be best to go. And one more thing, do not mention the name of Compeyson to your visitor. If that visitor discovers that this man is in London, he will never leave before he has tracked him down and—" Here Wemmick moved his hand across his throat in a cutting motion.

After Wemmick left, I stared into the fire as if I could see in the flames a method by which Magwitch could be smuggled out of the country. Herbert's entrance interrupted my thoughts. He had just come from visiting his beloved Clara, who lived with her invalid father beside the river. From his window, the old man enjoyed watching the passing ships.

As Herbert spoke, I had an inspiration. "That house is perfect! From there, we could row Magwitch out on the river and transfer him and me to a ship bound for anywhere. There are captains who will do anything for money and ask no questions."

Wemmick's Final Warning!

Herbert became enthusiastic about my plan at once. "You must buy a boat," he said. "We will row on the river every day until people around there get used to seeing us. Then on the day of the escape, there will be no comment on our rowing out as usual."

The next day I bought a boat, and Herbert and I started rowing. At first we did not stay out very long because we had to accustom our muscles to pulling an oar.

I sent Magwitch's purse of money back to him by Herbert. Later, by a roundabout route, I managed to visit him myself, feeling certain no one had been able to follow me.

I soon met Clara Barley, a sweet girl with a round, pretty face. Later, I congratulated Herbert on his choice, and he became red with happiness at my praise of Clara.

Magwitch was somewhat subdued by the need to switch his lodging. Though he protested feebly, I persuaded him that now was not the time to

Pip Buys a Rowboat.

draw attention to ourselves by investing in a showy carriage and horses. His protests were stronger at my plan to smuggle him out of London. But when he understood that I was coming with him, he became sensible and agreeable to everything.

He clasped my hand in both of his and held it until I had to leave. Of course, I gave no hint that I would separate from him once I got him safely away.

My financial situation was now very low, and I had to sell some jewelry. But this still wasn't enough to meet all my obligations, so without much hope, I decided to turn to Miss Havisham to pay off the contract with Clarriker's on Herbert's behalf.

On my way to the coach station, I stopped at Mr. Jaggers's office to tell him of my plan.

Jaggers nodded approval of my plan for Magwitch, but cautioned me, "Don't be in too much of a hurry. The best place to hide is in a big city like London."

Pip Sells His Jewelry.

Near the end of our conversation, Jaggers's servant, Molly, entered with his hot lunch. With her head down, she put the tray on a small table. As I rose to leave, I jostled the tray, and the soup splashed over its bowl a little. Molly's head came up angrily and her eyes flashed at me for a second. But that momentary flare of temper made me gasp, for I saw in Molly's eyes Estella's angry, contemptuous eyes, and in her nose and cheeks, features that were identical to Estella's!

When my conversation with Mr. Jaggers was over, I took Mr. Wemmick aside in the outer office and asked who Molly was.

"A murderess!" he whispered. "Jaggers was her lawyer and got her off. It was jealousy of her husband that caused the crime. She was supposed to have killed their child as well."

Pip Notices Familiar Features!

Molly Had Strangled Her Rival.

CHAPTER 14

Fire!

As the coach jolted me toward Miss Havisham's house, I went over again and again the story that Wemmick had confided in me. Molly had some gypsy blood in her, and when she imagined that her husband was being lured away by another woman, she had strangled that woman. Then, as revenge on her husband, Wemmick said, she was supposed to have also killed their child.

I knew this was not so, for Estella had to be that child. I could not be mistaken in recognizing the origins of those eyes I had loved for so long. Molly had to be Estella's mother and had probably been glad to let Mr. Jaggers save her child from a life of poverty.

When I arrived at Miss Havisham's, she seemed to be older and weaker. She listened quietly to my explanation of the secret help I had given Herbert and my present inability to complete the contract. Then I told her, "The sum I need is nine hundred pounds."

Miss Havisham was not shocked. Instead, she looked into the fire and said in a dreamy, faraway voice, "His father, Matthew Pocket, once gave me some advice. I did not take it, and I have been unhappy ever since . . . ." Then she roused herself and added sharply, "If I give you the money, will you promise to keep it a secret from the Pockets?"

I gave her my promise, and she wrote a short note to Mr. Jaggers, instructing him to pay out the money from her account. I took the note and thanked her.

Then as I turned to go, she called to me in a trembling voice, "You see how alone I am now? How she has deserted me?"

Pip Asks Miss Havisham for a Loan.

I answered quietly, "It could never have ended in any other manner." And though I had avoided reading the newspapers because I did not want to know when the wedding was to occur, I asked, "Is she married?"

As Miss Havisham nodded "yes," my face twisted in pain and heartbreak.

Then she gasped, and her cane fell from her hand. She spoke quietly. "I see in your face, Pip, a face exactly like mine many years ago at twenty minutes to nine!"

I covered my face with my hands until I could regain my composure. Miss Havisham was moaning and weeping. When I looked at her again, she was rocking from side to side, crying, "What have I done? What have I done?"

I wanted to answer that she had ruined my life, but that would only be partly true. I, myself, had made many mistakes and had had many foolish hopes and dreams, many foolish great expectations.

A Broken Heart over Estella's Marriage

"Forgive me, Pip! Forgive me!" she pleaded, holding out her hands.

I went to her and took the aged, trembling hands in mine. "I do forgive you," I said.

She pressed my hands and would not let go. "I did not mean anything wicked in the beginning," she said. "I just wanted to keep Estella from ever suffering as I had suffered. But she began to grow into a beauty, and I praised her and gave her jewels and kept warning her against love. Soon there was only ice in her heart."

I detached my hands from hers and drew up a stool beside her. "Whose child is Estella?" I asked quietly.

She shook her head. "I don't know. At some point in my wasted life, I decided I wanted a little girl to love and keep safe from my fate. I told Mr. Jaggers, and he said he would look about for an orphan. One night, he arrived with a little girl of about two or three. I adopted her and called her Estella."

"Forgive me, Pip! Forgive me!"

We talked no more. I stayed with her as she fell into a light doze near the fireplace. Then I went downstairs and wandered about the house a bit, for I felt it was the last time I should see it.

Suddenly, a terrible scream reached my ears. I raced upstairs and found Miss Havisham's room on fire. She came tottering toward me, flames blazing from her wedding dress and veil. I tore off my coat and wrapped her in it to smother the flames. She struggled against me, but I held her down, trying at the same time to beat out the flames licking at her hair. All the while, she kept crying, "Tell her I forgive her! Tell her I forgive her!"

Servants burst in and fought the fire. The doctor was sent for, and Miss Havisham was found to be alive but unconscious.

After treating my badly burned hands, the doctor said there was nothing more I could do there, so I returned to London the next day.

Flames Blaze from Miss Havisham's Dress.

Herbert Bandages Pip's Hand.

CHAPTER 15

Secrets from the Past

I was still in a state of shock when I reached home. Herbert rebandaged my hands and made me lie down. I could move the fingers of my right hand in spite of the wrapping, but my left hand had to be kept perfectly still. The doctor had made me carry it in a sling. In spite of the pain, I still had many errands to do. But I felt feverish, so Herbert insisted on attending to some of the errands for me. He notified his father and Miss Havisham's other relatives of what had happened. He also notified Estella, who was in Paris, at an address furnished by Mr. Jaggers.

But despite Herbert's help, there were still matters that only I could attend to. When I felt a little stronger, I went to Mr. Jaggers and gave him Miss Havisham's note. He made out a check for nine hundred pounds to Clarriker, and sent a messenger asking him to meet me at Jaggers's office.

Clarriker arrived and accepted the final payment called for by our contract. He explained that the shipping business was expanding faster every day, and that Herbert would soon be made a full partner. "But first," he insisted, "Herbert will be sent to the East to open up and take charge of one of our branch offices."

After Clarriker left us, Jaggers called me aside. "No names now, but it is time for any visitor from New South Wales to leave London. The authorities are circling in too close."

When I returned home and told Herbert what Jaggers had advised, we both looked at my bandaged hands in despair. I could not row!

Pip Makes the Final Payment to Clarriker.

Finally Herbert came up with a solution. "We shall enlist the aid of Startop."

Startop had been the third student tutored by Herbert's father along with myself and the hateful Drummle. Startop was honest and dependable, and agreed to help us.

Watchful of being followed, we went to Clara Barley's house by the river to alert Magwitch. He was shocked to see me bandaged, and was more concerned with any pain I might have suffered than with the escape plan.

"Oh, dear boy, I don't deserve your goodness," said Magwitch. "You are dearer to me than a son, which I never had . . . dearer even than the daughter I did once have."

"You never spoke of a child," I said. "Where is she now?"

"It's a terrible story," he began with a deep sigh, "but you two deserve to know everything about me. I'll just light my pipe before I begin." He filled it with the evil-smelling tobacco he favored, though I had offered to get him some of the best

Magwitch Is Shocked To See Pip Hurt.

that London imported. Then he began. "Now, I don't know who my parents were. I only know that I was in and out of jail all my life. But I was married at one time—a young gypsy woman, or part gypsy, she was. We had a little girl. My wife was hot tempered, and one day she choked to death another woman she thought I fancied."

He stopped and seemed to be thinking about those two women, who, so many years ago, had contended for his love. He roused himself and continued. "My wife was so angry with me that she told me she was going to kill our little girl. She disappeared with the child before I could do anything.

"The next thing I knew, she was arrested and ordered to stand trial for murdering that woman, which she certainly had done. But Mr. Jaggers took over her defense. That was how I got to know his name. I disappeared then, because otherwise I would have had to testify that my wife had killed our little girl too.

Magwitch's Wife Threatened Their Child.

"It was not until a long time later that I heard that Mr. Jaggers had got my wife off. Wonderful, clever man, is Mr. Jaggers. But he couldn't have done it if they had known about the child being killed as well. So, Pip, you are my child now."

It was fortunate that my burns had caused my face to be drawn and pale. Otherwise Herbert and Magwitch would surely have noticed the powerful effect the story had on me—so powerful that I was unable to speak a word.

Magwitch's pipe had gone out, and now he relit it and went on. "After all these years I don't hate my wife for what she done anymore. There's only one person I hate, and that's the one I was fighting on the marshes back in the time when I first seen my boy here." Magwitch reached over and patted my knee.

I managed to nod and smile at him, though my head still whirled at his story.

"That wicked man used me," continued Magwitch. "He appeared to be something of a gentleman; he would plan a crime and I would carry it

Jaggers Got Magwitch's Wife Off.

out. That way, he was safe and dry, while I was the one in danger. He also took most of the money we made, since he said that it was his brains that figured how to get it, and that my strong back and daring could be replaced easily.

"Then the time came when we was caught. Right off, he demanded separate trials, and he give evidence against me, saying I had forced him into crime. With the court seeing this nice-spoken, well-dressed gentleman a-talking against me—who looked well, you see me before you—who were they going to believe? So I went to prison and *he* went free. I swore to get my revenge.

"When I got out, his wife told me where he was. He was down in Kent, tricking some rich woman out of her money. I chased him then, and many times after. When I found him on the marshes, Pip, I could have gone free, but I wouldn't have Compeyson go free too. I wanted him in jail."

Compeyson Betrayed Magwitch.

Herbert gave a start when Magwitch mentioned Compeyson's name, but he said nothing.

When we left Magwitch, both of us started talking eagerly at once. My voice was louder, and I got to tell my story first. I told Herbert about Molly and the information Wemmick had given me about her, and joined her story to Magwitch's story. "So Magwitch is Estella's father," I concluded. "But it would do no one any good to have it known."

Herbert agreed, and we swore to keep it a secret. Then he began, "This man Compeyson—"

I interrupted him to offer, "He is in London, but Magwitch must not know. So I did not mention his name to you after Mr. Wemmick told me about him."

"What I was about to say," said Herbert, finally getting a word in "is that Compeyson was Miss Havisham's beloved!"

Pip and Herbert Exchange Stories.

Inquiring About Foreign Steamers

CHAPTER 16

Rowing Toward Freedom

Wednesday, two days away, was set for Magwitch's escape. On Monday and Tuesday, Herbert and I made inquiries about the foreign steamers that would be leaving at a time when our rowboat could meet up with them. We settled on one bound for Hamburg, Germany, and found out what she looked like.

The plan was to row down the Thames River to Clara's house. When Magwitch saw us coming, he would come down the stone steps to the river. It was necessary to go downriver on a previous tide and lie in wait for our steamer to approach.

Startop and Herbert would row and I would steer. Startop was not taken into our confidence and was only told that this was just a secret little outing we were indulging in.

While I secured passports with the help of Mr. Jaggers, Herbert alerted Startop and Magwitch. Both Herbert and I had a feeling of being watched, but could detect no one following us. We were probably overly nervous.

Wednesday was one of those March days when it feels like summer in the sun and winter in the shade. Herbert and I wore heavy jackets, and I took a bag with toilet articles and a few changes of clothes. Where I was going or what I might do there were questions I did not think about. Magwitch's safety was my only concern for now. As I went out the door of our rooms, I turned for a last look. I would probably never see them again.

Startop was waiting by my boat, and we cast off at 8:30 A.M. Soon we were part of the river traffic of coal barges, steamers, oyster boats, and rowboats like ours, with their occupants out for

Pip Packs His Bag.

pleasure or exercise. We intended to row with the tide until it turned at three. Then we would continue on, rowing against it until dark. This would take us somewhere between Kent and Essex, where the river is broad and solitary. We would put up overnight in some isolated inn, then wait for our Hamburg steamer, which would be starting from London with the tide about 9:00 A.M. on Thursday.

As we rowed toward the stone steps by Clara's house, we saw Magwitch coming down to meet us. He wore a cloak and carried a black canvas bag— an outfit which made him look like a river-pilot. We pulled over quickly, and Herbert gave him a hand on board.

Magwitch put an arm on my shoulder and said, "Faithful dear boy, that was well done. Thank you, thank you."

I pressed his hand and looked nervously about to see if anyone was watching him board. Everything seemed normal, so we proceeded downriver.

Magwitch Comes To Meet the Boat.

Magwitch smoked his pipe and was the least anxious of us all.

At nightfall, we came opposite a rundown inn. The innkeeper and his wife looked like villains, yet they served a good and generous meal, which we ate by the fireplace.

Herbert and Startop, who now knew of the escape plan, were tired out from their day of rowing and slept heavily. I shared a room with Magwitch, for I didn't like to have him out of my sight. I slept with most of my clothes on and woke several times during the night, thinking I heard men's voices. The last time I heard these voices, I looked out the window. In the moonlight I could see the pier where we had tied our boat. Two men were looking in it, but then they continued onto the marsh without a glance toward the inn. I guessed that they were customs inspectors.

The next morning, we were up early and back in the boat. We stayed in a sheltered part of the bank until 1:30, when we saw the smoke of the Hamburg steamer. Magwitch and I readied

Stopping for Dinner at a River Inn

ourselves and our two bags. I shook hands with Startop and Herbert. Neither Herbert's eyes nor my own were quite dry.

As we rowed out into the path of the steamer bearing down on us, another rowboat from another spot on the bank did the same. The rowers drew alongside us, leaving just enough room for the play of the oars. Aside from the rowers, there was one man steering and yet another sitting wrapped in a cloak and whispering instructions to the steerer.

The man in the cloak hailed us. "You have a returned convict with you! I order Abel Magwitch to surrender, and I order you to assist in apprehending him!"

At the same moment, his rowers pulled ahead and in front of us, blocking our way. Hands reached out and held our boat fast to theirs. This caused great confusion aboard the steamer, with some voices calling to us and others commanding their paddles to stop. Yet the steamer still bore down on us.

Waiting For the Hamburg Steamer

GREAT EXPECTATIONS

The steersman in the rowboat leaned into our boat and laid his hand on Magwitch's shoulder. But Magwitch leaned across and pulled the cloak away from the man who was giving orders. The face that was revealed was that of the other convict I had seen on the marshes in my boyhood! It was Compeyson!

Terror-stricken, Compeyson lurched backward as Magwitch threw himself from our boat onto him, tossing them both into the water. In the process, Magwitch capsized our boat.

I was in the water only a few moments when I was pulled into the other rowboat. Herbert was pulled in next, then Startop. I looked about frantically and spotted Magwitch feebly swimming. The rowers spotted him too and hauled him on board, chaining him at the wrists and ankles.

Our escape had failed!

Magwitch Throws Himself on Compeyson.

Magwitch Is Seriously Injured.

CHAPTER 17

Magwitch's "Dear Boy"

Magwitch was breathing with difficulty because of a wound in his chest. He had received that wound and a deep cut on his head when the Hamburg steamer had swept over him.

I cradled him in my arms and, in whispered gasps, he explained that he and Compeyson had gone into the water locked in each other's arms. There was a struggle and Magwitch had broken free.

The boat circled and circled the area where Compeyson was last seen, but he was nowhere to be found. His body was later recovered along the bank.

At length, we rowed back to the inn, and I was allowed to buy dry clothes for Magwitch. But the officer in charge—the one who had hailed us and steered their boat—said that all the prisoner's possessions, including his wet clothes and his money must be taken back to London and turned over to the authorities. Knowing that this would break Magwitch's heart, I made up my mind to keep that information from him.

Sitting beside the wounded Magwitch, I held his hand and urged him to conserve his strength. But he needed to speak.

"Dear boy," he said, "I knew I was taking a chance coming back to England. But I had to see you. I did, and now I'm content. My boy can be a gentleman without me. But it's best that a gentleman seem to have no connection with the likes of me. Just maybe sit in the courtroom where I can see you, and I don't ask for more."

The Law Takes Magwitch's Possessions.

"No!" I cried. "I will never stir from your side as long as they permit me to be with you! Please God, I will be as true to you as you have been to me!"

I felt his hand tremble in mine as I said this. Soon, smiling, he fell asleep.

Magwitch's trial was very short and very clear. Mr. Jaggers acted in his defense, but he warned me that the matter was hopeless. Even though he introduced testimony that Magwitch had reformed and had become a respected and wealthy man in New South Wales, the fact remained that he was a returned convict who had been warned not to return under punishment of death.

Because of his chest wound and exposure in the water, Magwitch grew weaker every day. As he faced his jury with ebbing strength, they could take no pity on him, but had to follow the law and find him guilty.

When the judge sentenced him to death, Magwitch said to him, "My Lord, I have received

Jaggers Defends Magwitch.

my sentence of death from the Almighty, but I bow to your sentence."

I earnestly hoped and prayed that he might die before the judge's sentence could be carried out. But, dreading that he might linger on, I wrote appeal after appeal, setting forth his whole story and mine to everyone in authority who might help, and followed up these petitions with personal visits.

I was able to visit Magwitch daily in the prison hospital. He was sinking slowly and hardly spoke at all. But he would respond to me by a slight pressure on my hand as I held his weak one. On my tenth visit, I saw that a change had come over him. His eyes were turned toward the door and lit up as I entered.

"Dear boy," he whispered, "you are always the first visitor into the ward."

"I wait by the gate, so that when they open it, I won't miss a minute of time with you."

"Thank you, dear boy, and God bless you!" he whispered. "You've never deserted me!"

Pip Writes Appeals for Magwitch.

I pressed his hand in silence, for I could not forget that I had once meant to desert him.

"And what's best of all," he continued "you've seemed closer to me since I came under this dark cloud than when the sun shone. That's worth everything to me."

He began to breathe with great difficulty, and a film seemed to come over his face.

"Are you in much pain?" I asked softly.

"I don't complain, dear boy."

Those were his last words. He made a weak gesture with his hand, and I understood that he wanted me to lay my hand on his breast. I did so, and he smiled and covered my hand with both of his.

The bell sounding the end of visiting hours rang just as the prison doctor entered. He leaned over Magwitch and shook his head sadly. Then he put a hand on my shoulder, indicating that I should remain in my seat.

I understood that Magwitch was living his last moments, and I leaned over him. "Dear

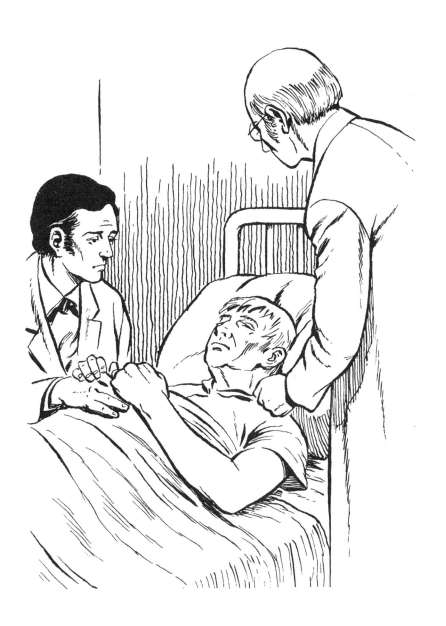

Magwitch Is Dying.

Magwitch," I whispered, fighting back the tears. "I must tell you something now, at this last moment. Can you understand me?"

He pressed my hand weakly to indicate that he did.

"You had a child once, whom you lost."

There was a stronger pressure on my hand.

"She was not killed, as you feared. She lived and found powerful friends. She is living now. She is a lady and very beautiful. And I am in love with her!"

With a last effort, Magwitch raised my hand to his lips and kissed it. Then he let it sink back on his breast, again covered by his hands. A placid look came over his face, and his head dropped quietly to one side. Magwitch was dead.

I was not horrified by witnessing death so closely. I felt as peaceful as the silent, aged face on the pillow, for while I had not been true to Joe Gargery and his friendship, I had found the strength of heart to be true to Magwitch and remain his "dear boy" to the end.

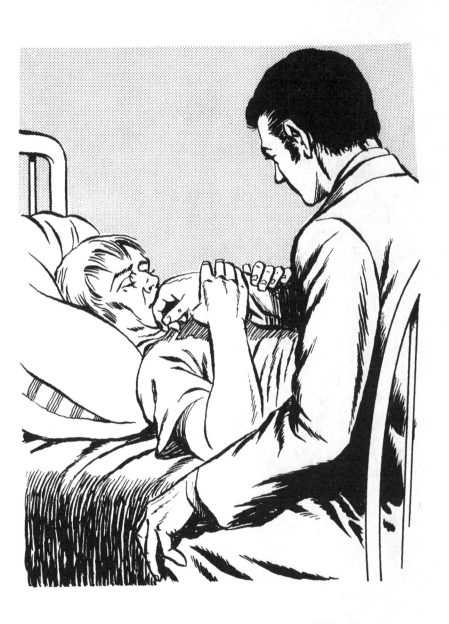

Magwitch's Last Act — a Kiss!

Pip Sublets His Rooms.

CHAPTER 18

Many Changes

When I was finally able to turn my attention back to my own affairs, I found them in terrible shape: I was heavily in debt, and I had to sublet my expensive rooms until the end of my lease. Herbert had already gone east to manage Clarriker's new branch office in Cairo, Egypt, but before leaving, he had assured me that a position of some kind would always exist for me at that branch.

However, I could make no decisions about my life for I was becoming ill. For weeks I had felt that some serious illness was trying to claim me, but I had fought it off until Magwitch died. Now a fever came on me, and I ached all over my body. I lay in bed shivering. But from time to time I would summon great strength in a delirium and wander in the streets. I came to my senses one day, still hot with fever, to find two men looking down at me as I lay in the street outside my house.

"Who are you? What do you want?" I called out hoarsely.

"Well, sir," said one of them, "we've come to arrest you for debt."

I groaned and attempted to get up. But my legs buckled under me. "I would come with you if I could," I said. "But you see how ill I am.

They went across the street and argued with one another, but ended by leaving. I stumbled into the house and relapsed into fever and nightmares. All the people I had known in my life seemed to be sitting, one after another, at my bedside. I talked and screamed and threw up, and gradually the variety of people disappeared,

Wandering in the Streets, Delirious!

leaving only one person always by my bed—Joe. The hand that sponged my hot face with cool water always seemed to be Joe's. The face that looked at me with a tender expression always seemed to be Joe's.

Finally I asked, weakly, "*Is* it Joe?"

And Joe's welcome voice answered, "That it is, dear old Pip."

I began to cry wildly, not in a delirium, but in my right senses. "Joe, you should be angry with me! Strike me, Joe! Tell me how I betrayed our friendship! Don't be so good to me!"

But Joe was so happy that I recognized him that he knelt beside the bed and gave me a hug. "You and me was always friends, dear old Pip," he said, his own eyes filling with tears. "Now be calm and get well."

Joe had been nursing me for a month. How long I was sick before that, I don't remember. Slowly I regained my strength, and it was like the old days in the house on the marshes. I fancied I was little

Joe Nurses Pip Back to Health.

Pip again, for Joe talked to me with the old simplicity and cared for me in the old protective way.

One afternoon, when Joe judged me strong enough, he told me that Miss Havisham had died of her burns. As expected, all her money was left to Estella. Now that the subject had arisen, I offered to tell him about my own great expectations and my benefactor, since it was obviously not Miss Havisham.

Joe broke in to say he had heard something about various events, but that it was an unnecessary subject between friends. Then he jumped up to prepare our evening meal, so ending that discussion.

When it became apparent that I had almost completely recovered, Joe left. He stole away early one morning, leaving a smudged and badly spelled note of farewell. Biddy had taught him to read and write, and he had been very proud to tell me this.

Enclosed in the note was a paid receipt for the debt for which I had been arrested. It was in Joe's

A Farewell Note and a Paid Bill

name. Up to this moment, I had not let myself think about this creditor, hoping that he had withdrawn court proceedings until I was better. I never dreamed that Joe had paid him his money.

I sat down, still with Joe's note and the receipt in my hand, and thought about my foolish, selfish life of recent years. Then I remembered the clean, clear air that would blow up from the river and over the marshes where I had been raised. The sweet face of sensible Biddy kept presenting itself to me. She had been my friend and confidante since her arrival after my sister's attack.

"What better way is there to change my life than marry Biddy?" I asked myself. "I will show her how humble and repentant I am. I will ask her to be my wife and to make the decision as to our future. If she wants me to work at the forge with Joe, I will do so. Or if she wishes me to find some occupation in the village or in the country, then I will do that. I will tell her of Herbert's offer, and if she wishes us to go to Egypt, that is what we will do."

Pip Decides To Ask Biddy to Marry Him.

GREAT EXPECTATIONS

Three days later, I took the coach to Kent. The June weather was delicious. The sky was blue, and the larks were soaring high over the green corn. As I neared the forge, I didn't hear the clink of Joe's hammer. As I came abreast of it, a shudder of fear went through me, for it was closed.

The house, however, was not deserted, for I saw fresh white curtains fluttering out the open window of the parlor. I hurried to the window and looked in. Joe and Biddy were standing arm in arm. They shouted with joy to see me and ran to embrace me. Biddy looked so fresh and pleasant that I embraced her again.

"Now that you are here, dearest Pip," she said, "my wedding day is quite perfect. Joe and I have just been married!"

I managed to congratulate them without showing them my disappointment. I then spent several hours with them before tearing myself away from these two dear people and hurrying back to London. There, I sold all I had and arranged to pay my creditors little by little.

Biddy and Joe's Wedding Day

Then I travelled to Egypt and took a position as a clerk in Clarriker & Company. Herbert had married Clara, and I lived with them. Gradually I rose in the firm, paid all my debts, and lived well within my means. I wrote constantly to Joe and Biddy. After several years, I became a partner in Clarriker's.

Our firm was never one of the largest, but we made a profit and had a good reputation. One day, Clarriker could not bear to keep the secret of Herbert's partnership any longer, and he told Herbert how it had come about. By now, Herbert's ability would have brought him a partnership on his own, but my money had done it when he needed it. And he loved me for it.

Pip Lives with the Pockets in Egypt.

A Little Pip!

CHAPTER 19

Eleven Years Later

It was eleven years before I returned to England. It was an evening in December, an hour or so after dark, when I quietly pushed open the kitchen door of the house on the marshes. There, smoking his pipe by the fire, was Joe, only a little gray. And opposite him, sitting on my own old little stool, was—a little Pip!

Joe jumped up to welcome me back and kept touching me to make sure it was really me. But the little boy hung back. Biddy rushed in and cried and kissed me.

GREAT EXPECTATIONS

After a few days, young Pip—for he had been named after me—and I became friends. We went for walks on the marshes, and I showed him my family's tombstones. To understand his thoughts and feelings, I had only to remember my own at his age in this place.

By the time I left, Pip was as attached to me as I had been to Joe when I was young. He stood by the forge and waved and waved until I was out of sight.

Before I left for London, I went to visit the site of Miss Havisham's house. Nothing of the burned-out house remained; only the garden was there, pushing wildly into the space once occupied by the house. I went through the old gate, no longer locked, and sat on a stone bench. Thoughts of Estella came rushing to me. I had heard that her life with Bentley Drummle had been most unhappy, unhappy enough to cause her to leave him. And I had heard that he had been killed in a riding accident soon after. But that had been two years years ago, and perhaps she had since

Showing Little Pip the Family's Grave

remarried. I wandered farther back in the garden, which looked stripped and desolate in the winter air. The figure of a woman stood forlornly in the moonlight, and, hearing my footsteps, she turned. We recognized one another at the same time.

"Estella!" I cried out and rushed to her.

"I am greatly changed, Pip," she said softly. "It is a wonder that you recognized me."

The youthful freshness was indeed gone, but she had kept the majesty and charm of her beauty. Her proud eyes were changed also and now held a soft, saddened look. We sat down on a bench, and I asked if she came here often.

"No. I came here tonight for the first time, to say good-bye to the place. This property was my last possesion, and I have sold it. Do you still live abroad, Pip?"

I told her of my partnership with Clarriker and Company, and she seemed pleased.

"I have thought of you often," said Estella.

"For a time, I could not bear to think of you— of your love that I had thrown away in my

A Chance Meeting

ignorance. But now I have given it a place in my heart." She smiled gently.

"You have always had a place in my heart," I said, taking her hand in mine.

We sat in silence for a time, then in a low voice, Estella said, "My suffering all these years has come to be a stronger teacher to me than all other teachers. I have been bent and broken, but I hope into a better shape. Since I must part from you again, I am glad that our parting is taking place here, in a place that I must also part with. I hope you have forgiven me and will be as considerate of me as you once were, and that we shall part as friends."

"We *are* friends," I said firmly. "As for parting, that remains to be seen."

We rose from the bench, her hand still in mine, and walked slowly away together, leaving the shadow of Miss Havisham behind.

Leaving Miss Havisham's Shadow Behind